This book belongs to:

....

Jane

Dwayne

For Sam Day - A.S.

To Carla and Vera - M.O.

HODDER CHILDREN'S BOOKS
First published in Great Britain in 2018 by Hodder and Stoughton
This edition published in 2019 by Hodder and Stoughton

A CIP catalogue record for this book is available from the British Library.

ISBN: 978 1 444 93345 1

1 3 5 7 9 10 8 6 4 2

Printed and bound in China

Hodder Children's Books
An imprint of Hachette Children's Group
Part of Hodder and Stoughton
Carmelite House, 50 Victoria Embankment, London, EC4Y 0DZ

An Hachette UK Company
www.hachette.co.uk
www.hachettechildrens.co.uk

ANDY STANTON   MIGUEL ORDÓÑEZ

h

Hodder Children's Books

GOING TO THE VOLCANO

Going off with Jane-o
to look at the volcano!

Going off with Jane-o
to look at the volcano!

Walking down the lane-o
to look at the volcano!

Walking down the lane-o to look at the volcano!

Riding the Great Dane-o

Riding the Great Dane-o

to look at the **volcano!**

to look at the **volcano!**

Sitting on the train-o
to look at the **volcano!**

Jumping on the plane-o
to look at the **volcano!**

Jumping on the plane-o
to look at the volcano!

Splashing through the rain-o
to look at the **volcano!**

Splashing through the rain-o
to look at the **volcano!**

Going up the crane-o

to look at the
volcano!

Climbing down
the chain-o
to look at the
volcano!

In a lot of pain-o
because of the volcano!

In a lot of pain-o
because of the **volcano!**

NEVER do it again-o.

STAY OFF THE
VOLCANO!

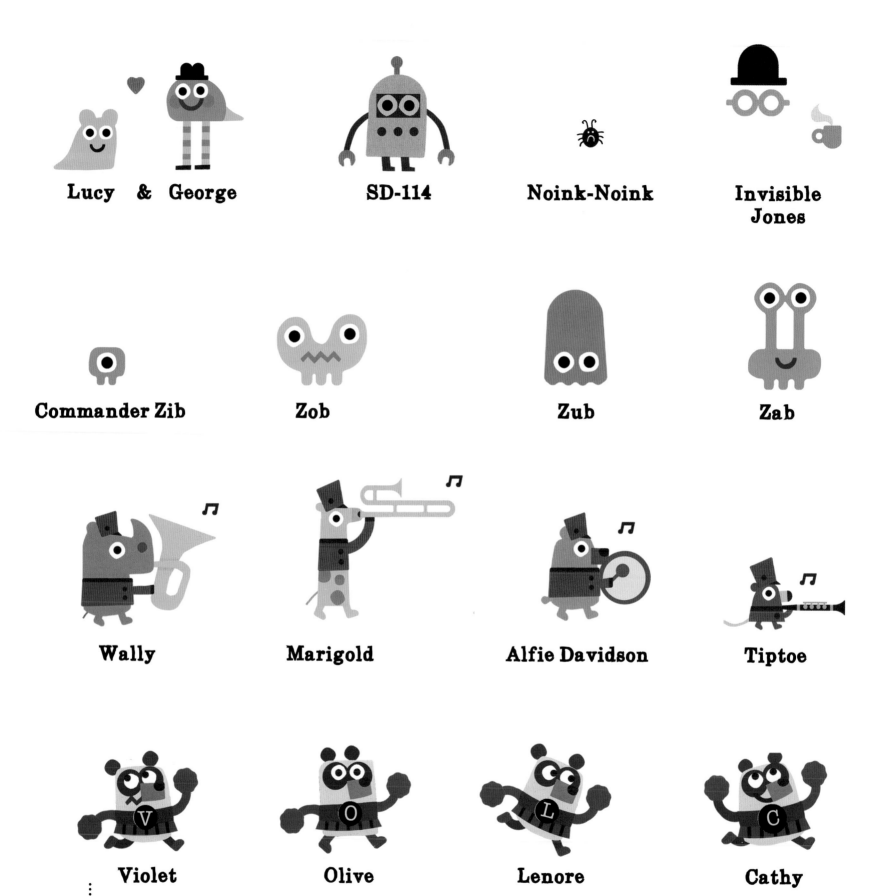

Lucy & George

SD-114

Noink-Noink

Invisible Jones

Commander Zib

Zob

Zub

Zab

Wally

Marigold

Alfie Davidson

Tiptoe

Violet

Olive

Lenore

Cathy

THE LAVA GIRLS

El pájaro de Miguel

Roger, the incredible colour-changing cat

Clumsy Michael

Anxiety Man

Commander Zib's wife, Zoob

Dr Eyjafjallajökull

Nurse Erebus

Boomer

Baby Boomer

Nurse Etna

Dr Vesuvius

Andrea

Nicole

Trevor

Dr Krakatoa